THE LABYRINTH OF DOOM

ALSO BY
STUART GIBBS

THE FUNJUNGLE SERIES

Belly Up

Poached

Big Game

Panda-monium

Lion Down

Tyrannosaurus Wrecks

Bear Bottom

THE SPY SCHOOL SERIES

Spy School

Spy Camp

Evil Spy School

Spy Ski School

Spy School Secret Service

Spy School Goes South

Spy School British Invasion

Spy School Revolution

Spy School at Sea

Spy School Project X

Spy School the Graphic Novel
(with Anjan Sarkar)

THE MOON BASE ALPHA SERIES

Space Case

Spaced Out

Waste of Space

THE CHARLIE THORNE SERIES

*Charlie Thorne
and the Last Equation*

Charlie Thorne and the Lost City

*Charlie Thorne and
the Curse of Cleopatra*

THE ONCE UPON A TIM SERIES

Once Upon a Tim

The Last Musketeer

THE LABYRINTH OF DOOM

ONCE UPON A TIM

BOOK 2

WITHDRAWN

STUART GIBBS

ILLUSTRATED BY STACY CURTIS

SIMON & SCHUSTER BOOKS FOR YOUNG READERS

NEW YORK   LONDON   TORONTO   SYDNEY   NEW DELHI

SIMON & SCHUSTER BOOKS FOR YOUNG READERS

An imprint of Simon & Schuster Children's Publishing Division

1230 Avenue of the Americas, New York, New York 10020

SIMON & SCHUSTER BOOKS FOR YOUNG READERS

and related marks are trademarks of Simon & Schuster, Inc.

For information about special discounts for bulk purchases, please contact Simon & Schuster Special Sales at 1-866-506-1949 or business@simonandschuster.com.

The Simon & Schuster Speakers Bureau can bring authors to your live event. For more information or to book an event, contact the Simon & Schuster Speakers Bureau at 1-866-248-3049 or visit our website at www.simonspeakers.com.

The text for this book was set in Adobe Caslon Pro.

Manufactured in the United States of America

0922 LAK

First Edition

2 4 6 8 10 9 7 5 3 1

Library of Congress Cataloging-in-Publication Data

Names: Gibbs, Stuart, 1969– author.

Title: The labyrinth of doom / Stu Gibbs.

Description: First Simon & Schuster Books for Young Readers hardcover edition. | New York : Simon & Schuster Books for Young Readers, 2021. | Series: Once upon a Tim ; book 2 | Audience: Ages 7–10 | Audience: Grades 2–3 | Summary: "Tim and his friends must face The Labyrinth of Doom on their latest quest"— Provided by publisher.

Identifiers: LCCN 2021016530 (print) | LCCN 2021016531 (ebook) | ISBN 9781534499287 (paper-over-board) | ISBN 9781534499300 (ebook)

Subjects: CYAC: Knights and knighthood—Fiction. | Quests (Expeditions)—Fiction. | Fantasy. | LCGFT: Novels.

Classification: LCC PZ7.G339236 Lab 2021 (print) | LCC PZ7.G339236 (ebook) | DDC [Fic]—dc23

LC record available at https://lccn.loc.gov/2021016530

LC ebook record available at https://lccn.loc.gov/2021016531

THE
LABYRINTH
OF
DOOM

CHAPTER ONE

How I Started My Day

ONCE UPON A TIME...

...it wasn't easy to be a knight-in-training.

My name is Tim. I'm a junior member of the Knight Brigade for the Great and Glorious Kingdom of Merryland.

I don't really know you, but I'm guessing your normal morning goes something like this:

Wake up.

Go to the bathroom.

Shower. (Maybe.)

Get dressed.

Eat breakfast.

Go to school.

Now, here's what *I* do on a typical morning:

Wake up.

Face *this*:

That's right. I started my day by squaring off against a *dragon*.

My head instructor, Sir Vyval, leader of the Brave and Honorable Knights of Merryland, believes that a knight must be prepared to defend himself at any moment. Even if that moment happens to be very, very early in the morning. So he will occasionally do something to keep me on my toes, like releasing a fire-breathing dragon into my room while I'm asleep. If I defeat the dragon, I pass the test. If the dragon defeats *me* . . . well, Sir Vyval needs to find a new knight to train.

Do you know what it's like to wake up facing a dragon? It stinks.

Literally. You probably know that dragons are foul-tempered and are covered with scales and breathe fire, but people rarely talk about the fact that they smell like a dead fish that someone kept in their armpit for a week.

Also, it's quite scary.

I will admit, the first thing I did upon seeing a dragon staring at me was shriek in fear.

But then, I'm only twelve years old.

The second thing I did was roll off the pile of hay I was sleeping on in the knights' barracks at the castle. (People in my time don't have beds unless they are royals; we sleep on piles of hay, if we're lucky enough to find it. And if we're not lucky enough to find hay, we sleep on things like dirt or gravel.) Then I grabbed the sword and shield that I have learned to keep by my side at all times. Which turned out to be a very wise decision, as the dragon released a blast of fire, which I was able to deflect like this:

Dragons can't blast you with flame *forever.* Eventually they have to stop to recharge. So when this one did, I took my sword and . . .

Oh.

I just realized what you're thinking.

You're thinking, *That's only a baby dragon! The way this*

kid was narrating, I thought he was fighting a real dragon. That puny little thing doesn't look that dangerous at all.

Well, you're wrong.

A baby dragon is *plenty* dangerous. It's not like I was fighting a *rabbit* here. Baby dragons might be smaller than adult dragons, but they still have bad attitudes, sharp teeth, nasty claws, and the whole breathing-fire thing. Make one false move around a baby dragon and it will fricassee your butt.

This one was particularly unpleasant. It kept trying to claw me, bite me, and flame-broil me. I had to fend it off repeatedly with my sword and my shield.

However, there is one thing you can do to a baby dragon that you can't do to an adult.

This:

Try kicking an adult dragon in the rear end and you'll break all your toes. And then you'll get eaten.

But this worked. Once I booted him out the window, the little jerk decided he'd had enough and flew off to roost in one of the castle turrets.

A moment later, Sir Vyval entered my room.

Sir Vyval was revered throughout the land as one of the bravest, most dashing knights. He was heavily scarred from many storied battles. He had lost two fingers in the Orc Wars. He had lost an eye in the Battle of the Basilisks. And he had lost his nose in a fight against a giant manticore.

He also lost his temper a lot. Sir Vyval might have been a great knight who had served the kingdom with honor for many years, but he wasn't very nice or understanding. You never wanted to make him angry.

I looked to him expectantly.

"That," he said, "was absolutely terrible."

My spirits sagged. "Really?" I asked. "Because I managed to fend the dragon off without so much as a scratch."

"You *barely* managed to fend off a baby dragon," Sir Vyval said dismissively. "If I had fought like that in the

Great Dragon Uprising, this whole kingdom would have been burned to the ground! And it took you way too long to chase that little thing off. Your cousin Bull took care of the one I put in his room in half the time!"

My spirits sagged even more. Bull isn't really my cousin—and he isn't really a *he*. Bull is really my best friend, Belinda, who is pretending to be a boy so she can also become a knight. (In my time, peasant girls only have two career options: housewife or witch. Belinda didn't like either of those, so she chose to live a lie instead.) She had always been better at fighting, throwing axes, and stabbing things than I had, and now that she was training to be a knight, her skills were improving quickly. Just a few days before, Belinda had handily defeated Sir Cuss, one of the kingdom's most honored knights, in a practice fight.

"If you want to become a member of this force, you're going to have to do better," Sir Vyval told me. "Much, much, much, much, *much* better. Now get this room cleaned up. There's a dragon poop in the corner." With that, he stormed out and slammed the door behind him.

Like I said, training wasn't easy. The sun had barely risen, and I had already fought a dragon and been chewed out by my commander.

And the day only got worse from there.

A lot worse.

CHAPTER TWO

What Knight School Was Like

You are probably wondering to yourself, *If training to be a knight was so awful, then why was this knucklehead doing it?*

Because the alternative was even *more* awful.

I was born a peasant. All my ancestors were peasants. All my relatives were peasants.

I *hated* being a peasant. It was boring. It was exhausting. It was laborious. ⟨ IQ BOOSTER! | It was ...

Oh. You noticed that IQ Booster arrow. Every once in a while, as a favor to you, I like to use a big word. How is this a favor? Well, sometimes when you come across a book as exciting, thrilling, and hilarious as this one, your parents will frown on it because it has *illustrations*. Then they may suggest that you read something that's more educational, like *The Wonders of Mathematics* or *A Field Guide to Norwegian Spittlebugs*. But thanks to those IQ Boosters I've tossed in, you can tell your parents that this book *is* educational! For example, "laborious" means "extremely difficult" and "strenuous." (If your parents challenge you to use it in a sentence, say "Doing my chores this morning was really laborious, and now I'd like to relax by reading *The Labyrinth of Doom*.")

Anyhow . . .

Training to be a knight was also laborious, but being a knight had many advantages over being a peasant. Such as:

1) Knights got to live in the castle, rather than huts like peasants.

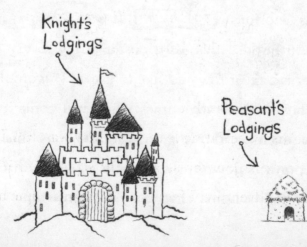

Knight's Lodgings

Peasant's Lodgings

2) Knights ate better than peasants. The royal family fed us delicious things like meat and fruit, while peasants ate gruel three times a day, every day, for their entire lives. Sometimes knights even got dessert, which was so rare for peasants that many people thought it was only a myth. Admittedly, when we got dessert, it was usually leftovers from the royal dinner, like chocolate cake with several bites taken out of it, but still ... IT WAS CHOCOLATE CAKE!!!! Which, if you've only had gruel your entire life, is the greatest thing ever.

And most importantly ...

3) Knights had exciting lives. Peasantry was dull. I had only been on one journey as a knight so far, and it had been nonstop adventure. I had gone on a great, epic quest

too, and rescued Princess Grace of Merryland after she
had been stolen by a stinx. True, I had nearly died several
times, but still, it had been the greatest, most incredible,
most fulfilling few days of my life. I was extremely eager
to have another great adventure someday soon . . .

Knight's
Work

Peasant's
Work

zzzZZ

...although Sir Vyval insisted I had a *lot* of training to do before that could happen.

I suppose another thing you might be wondering is: How did I get to go on a great, epic quest if I was only a knight-in-training?

The answer is that I was working for a different royal at the time. And I was a bit of a sucker.

You see, Prince Ruprecht, who is the only son of the royal family in the Kingdom of Wyld, where I grew up, recruited Belinda and me, along with Ferkle, our village idiot, to help him rescue Princess Grace, assuming she would fall in love with him. But it turned out that Prince Ruprecht was not the wonderful prince we had all assumed he was. Even though everyone in the Kingdom of Wyld thought that he was brave and valiant, he was really a cruel and devious coward. Ruprecht's even meaner and more devious adviser, Nerlim, had concocted an evil plan. They had Belinda, Ferkle, and me do all the hard work to save Princess Grace—and then tried to kill us so that we couldn't tell everyone the truth about Ruprecht.

Obviously they had not been successful. Belinda,

Ferkle, and I escaped—

and Princess Grace

realized that she

didn't need to fall in

love with any prince

who came along

and rescued her.

Princess Grace

then offered

us the chance

to become

knights for *her*

in Merryland.

Ferkle opted

out, as he enjoyed

being the village

idiot, but Belinda and I didn't want to go back to being

peasants. My parents were happy to let me go; since I was

twelve and it was the olden days, it was time for me to

leave home and start out on my own anyhow. (Belinda's

parents were happy too, although Belinda had lied to them about the whole learning-to-be-a-knight thing and told them she had been accepted as a student at the prestigious Madame Blackbottom's School of Witchcraft.) And so Belinda and I eagerly went off to become knights.

Although we hadn't known about all the training we'd have to do.

To be honest, I had never really thought that much about what the day-to-day life of a young knight would be like. I had expected there would be lots of quests and adventures, like the one I had just gone on. I had *not* counted on Sir Vyval routinely waking me by putting baby dragons in my bed.

There were plenty of other laborious training exercises as well:

Long runs through the countryside wearing heavy suits of armor.

Courses full of dangerous obstacles like swinging pen-
dulums and pits of fire, which we had to navigate wearing
heavy suits of armor.

Battles against other young dangerous beasts, like chimeras and harpies and blugworts, which of course had to be done in heavy armor.

And cleaning and polishing all the other knights' armor, which we had to do in our *own* heavy armor.

As you can see, a typical day could be extremely exhausting—and therefore, very soporific. ◁ IQ BOOSTER!

("Soporific" means "sleep inducing." If your parent challenges you to use it in a sentence, you could say, "I find educational books like *A Field Guide to Norwegian*

Spittlebugs to be much more soporific than exciting, hilarious tales like *The Labyrinth of Doom*.")

So I was really wiped out after a long morning of training. Which is why I *might* have nodded off for a tiny bit while I was on guard duty. Which led to quite a bit of trouble.

As you will see.

CHAPTER THREE

How We Got Captured

Normally, knights didn't do guard duty. That responsibility was for sentries. Sentries did things like patrolling the ramparts, staring off at things in the distance, and yelling "Halt! Who goes there?" to anyone who showed up at the castle gates.

But Sir Vyval and the other knights felt that Belinda and I should experience guard duty as part of our training. They *said* it was to teach us how to be alert and vigilant, but I think they really did it because they didn't like us very much.

After all, Belinda and I had successfully rescued Princess Grace from the stinx and returned her to her kingdom, while Sir Vyval and the other knights had not.

The Royal Knights of Merryland had all been shopping for armor in the neighboring Kingdom of Tinkerdink when that happened. When Grace had been swiped, the knights had been caught with their pants down. Literally.

Belinda and I had ended up making the older knights look bad. Princess Grace's parents, King and Queen Sunderfire, were normally very kind and benevolent rulers, but they had been quite upset to learn that their knights had all gone armor shopping at the same time, which was a serious lapse of judgment on Sir Vyval's part. They had chewed the knights out and refused to give them any scraps of half-eaten chocolate cake for seven days.

So the knights made life difficult for us every chance they got.

Sir Vaylance made us scrub the gunk off his weapons.

Sir Mount made us clean the stables.

Sir Render made us clean his dirty underwear.

Sir Fass made us run the obstacle course over and over.

Sir Cumference made us chase the baby dragons out of the rafters.

Sir Cuss just shouted a lot of bad words at us.

The only one who was nice to us was Sir Eberal, who was also the smartest and oldest knight. He didn't go to battle that much. Instead, he preferred to learn everything he could about the enemy by reading books and doing research and then figure out clever ways to defeat them, which might explain why he was the only knight in Merryland who had all the fingers, eyes, and noses he'd been born with.

Anyhow, being a sentry was even more dull than being a peasant. At least when you were a peasant, you had things to do. Sentries just stood around waiting for something to happen.

So I fell asleep.

Because I was so tired from all the other things I had been doing that day.

One moment I was standing at the front gates of the castle, doing my best to remain alert.

And the next I looked like this:

Eventually I woke up again. Thankfully none of the other knights had noticed me sleeping on the job, or they probably would have punished me severely for letting my guard down. I wasn't sure how long I'd been asleep, because wristwatches wouldn't be invented for another few centuries, but I hoped it wasn't long enough for something bad to happen.

It was.

Although I didn't find that out until later that evening, when Belinda and I were having dinner with Princess Grace.

That was another advantage of being a knight. You got to be friends with a princess. Grace often invited Belinda and me to dine with her, which was much more enjoyable than eating with the other knights, as Princess Grace was nicer, kinder, and better smelling and didn't pick her teeth with her sword. (I think that Grace enjoyed eating with us, too, because, to be honest, she didn't seem to have many friends. Princesses were usually only supposed to associate with other princesses, but they all lived quite far apart; the closest one to us was Princess Winifred in the Kingdom of Spatula, which was suffering from an ogre infestation. King and Queen Sunderfire felt that their daughter needed companionship—and they liked Belinda and me because we had rescued Grace—so they welcomed our presence in the castle.)

The meal was delicious, as usual. But then, when you've had nothing to eat but gruel all your life, *anything* is delicious. The palace chef was going through a bird phase, so we had roast pheasant, duck, pigeon, swan, peacock, flamingo, and ostrich.

By the way, that weird-looking creature down by my

feet is my fr-dog, Rover. He *used* to be a dog, but then the mean witch who lived next door to my parents' hut turned him into a frog. Sort of. Now he *looks* like a frog, but acts like a dog. He might be a bit slimy, but he's loyal and kind and trustworthy, which is more than I can say for a lot of people I've met.

Before we could completely stuff ourselves with food, Princess Grace announced that she had a surprise: a whole new kind of dessert. It was called an apple pie.

I know apple pie probably isn't new to *you*, but in the days of yore, there were still plenty of foods we hadn't encountered yet. Like pizza. Or gyros. Or wontons. (Although, contrary to popular belief, we *did* have sushi, but that was really just fish that we hadn't cooked properly.)

So I had never heard of apple pie before, but the moment a servant carried it in, I knew it was going to be delicious. It smelled better than anything else I had smelled in my life. (Which wasn't saying much, because most things in my time smell terrible. Even Princess Grace, who was the cleanest person I knew, was a bit rank.)

The pie tasted even better than it smelled. Each of us

had a huge slice—and Grace also slipped a little bit to Rover, who gobbled it down. The castle chef had outdone himself. He had baked some scrumptious desserts before, but this was the best. Even better than the chocolate cake. The apples were sweet and tart. The crust was flaky and buttery. The cinnamon was fresh. And there was just a hint of a flavor I had never had before.

"Mmmm," I said. "Is there some sort of secret ingredient in this pie? Something that's not apple or cinnamon or crust?"

"Oooh," Grace said. "I'm tasting it too. It has kind of a poison-y flavor?"

Belinda and I paused, forkfuls of pie halfway to our mouths.

"Poison-y?" I repeated.

"Yes," Grace said. "It's a little bit sweet and a little bit sour and a little bit deadly. You know, like a poison."

I began to feel nauseated, as though I had eaten something that wasn't good for me. And also because I was worried. "Are you saying that someone poisoned this pie?"

Grace gasped. "Oh dear! It must have been that apple seller who came by the castle this afternoon. I *knew* that she looked suspicious!"

In knight training we had actually studied what to do in case you were poisoned. (Knights are always ending up in some sort of danger. We also have to learn what to do if you are bitten by a chimera, set on fire, or eaten by a sea serpent. Lots of people quit simply upon hearing that these things are even possibilities while on the job.)

To get rid of the poison, you were supposed to stick a finger down your throat and make yourself throw up. I tried to do this, but I couldn't even lift my arms. They suddenly felt like they were made of steel.

Belinda was struggling to lift her arms too, and looking very worried as well. And yet she couldn't help but ask, "What was suspicious about this apple seller?"

"Well," Grace said, "she was just giving the apples away, which didn't seem like a very good model for a profitable business. Plus, she was a bit evasive when I asked her where the apples were from. And also, she had a mustache." She frowned, looking upset at herself. "Dang it! I should have never accepted those silly apples! Usually I don't even answer the gates when people show up. But whoever was supposed to be standing guard there today had fallen asleep on the job."

My stomach went queasy. And not only because I had been poisoned—but because *I* was the one who had fallen asleep on the job. And now *this* was happening.

"This is all my fault!" Princess Grace wailed sullenly. "I can be such a fiddly fluff-head sometimes! I can't believe I . . . ummmmmmffllllphphphmmm." And then she passed out, face-first into her pie.

"That's not good," Belinda said. And then she passed out into her pie too.

"Ribbit," Rover croaked, and then he passed out on the floor.

I looked over them all, feeling foolish and miserable and . . . really, really, really tired. Then my brain shut down, and I passed out too.

I *told* you this day would get worse.

CHAPTER FOUR

Don't Worry. We're Not Dead.

I woke to the sound of laughter. Evil, maniacal laughter. The kind that goes *Mwah-ha-ha-ha-ha!*

While I was happy to learn that I was not dead, the laughter was vexing. < IQ BOOSTER !

("Vexing" means "bothersome" or "annoying." Like a mosquito bite. Or too much homework. Or people who gargle in public.)

Also, I wasn't pleased to discover that my arms and legs were bound.

Then I noticed that Belinda was tied up right next to me, looking equally vexed.

And Rover was tied up next to her. He looked confused, which wasn't surprising, because dogs are confused for a significant portion of their lives.

What Dogs Are Feeling

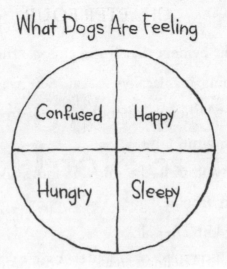

Confused | Happy
Hungry | Sleepy

Next to Rover was a large burlap sack filled with something around the size of a teenage human. I assumed the human-sized thing *was* a human, although I wasn't sure. I wondered if, perhaps, Princess Grace was inside.

Then Prince Ruprecht and Nerlim strode into view. It now became evident that Ruprecht was the one who had been laughing maniacally—because he was *still* laughing maniacally. Although he took a break from laughing to speak to us tauntingly.

"Well, well, well," he said. "It looks like you're all in quite a bit of trouble. I guess you're not the greatest knights in the kingdom after all."

"Ruprecht!" Belinda snarled. "And Smerkin! I should have known you were behind this!"

"Um . . . ," Nerlim said, looking like his feelings had been hurt. "My name's Nerlim. Not Smerkin."

"Whatever," Belinda said. "I forgot."

"You forgot?" Nerlim said with a gasp. "We went on a whole crusade together! And then I double-crossed you and revealed I had been deviously plotting against you the entire time! I tried to kill you! And you can't even remember my name?"

"Apparently not," Belinda said. "Besides, you look like a Smerkin."

Nerlim was obviously very upset by all this, but before

he could say anything, Prince Ruprecht cut him off. "It doesn't matter if you remember our names or not . . . ," he began.

"Easy for *you* to say," Nerlim muttered. "No one forgot *your* name."

". . . what's important here is that we have outwitted and captured you. And now we are going to get revenge for the horrible things you did to us!"

"Horrible things *we* did to *you*?" I echoed. "Nerlim just recounted how you plotted our deaths!"

"And then *you* left us in the lair of the stinx!" Ruprecht said accusingly. "While you brought Princess Grace home and stole all the credit for rescuing her from *me*!"

"But you *didn't* rescue her," I pointed out.

"Well, I doubt that you're going to rescue her this time either!" Ruprecht snapped. And then he burst into maniacal laughter again. "Mwah-ha-ha-ha-ha!"

I suddenly had a terrible sense of foreboding. < IQ BOOSTER!

("Foreboding" is a feeling that something bad will happen. Like the sense that you are going to fail a math test. Or forget to put your pants on before you leave the house. Or be forced to battle a dangerous, ferocious mythical beast—which somehow was actually the most likely scenario in my life.)

"Ruprecht, what have you done?" I asked.

"I have devised a new challenge to test your skills as knights," Ruprecht replied.

"Actually, *I* devised it," Nerlim grumbled under his breath. "Not that you'll even bother to remember my name."

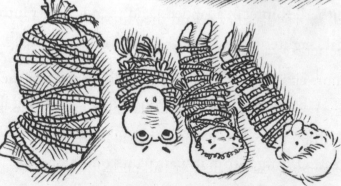

Ruprecht ignored this and went on. "After knocking all of you out with those poisoned apples, Smerkin and I brought you—"

"Nerlim!" Nerlim cried in exasperation.

"Right. Nerlim and I brought you here, to the Kingdom of Extravagancia, home of the most complex and dastardly labyrinth in the world! Not only is it an incredibly complicated maze that is impossible to find your way through, but it is also patrolled by bloodthirsty minotaurs, which will devour any humans they come across!"

Belinda gaped at him in surprise. "What? Why on earth would anyone build something like that?"

"It's one of those rivalries between kings that got a little out of hand," Ruprecht explained. "One king built a hedge maze at his castle. And then another king built a *better* hedge maze. And then another king built an even better maze and put a few baby dragons in it to make it more challenging. And on and on it went, until the King of Extravagancia built the world's most impossible labyrinth and filled it with minotaurs, just so he could say that his kingdom was the best. It's all perfectly understandable."

"No!" Belinda exclaimed. "It's not understandable *at all*! The poor peasants of these kingdoms are living in mud huts and eating gruel while the kings are throwing away their money by building giant mazes filled with bloodthirsty creatures that are half-man and half-bull! And why is something that's half-bull even bloodthirsty to begin with?! Bulls aren't carnivores! They eat grass!"

"Er . . . ," Ruprecht said. He glanced at Nerlim for some help, but Nerlim was pouting sullenly and didn't seem to want to participate. "I'm not really sure *why* they're blood-thirsty. That's just what I've heard."

"It has to do with the crossbreeding," said a voice from inside the burlap sack. A very thoughtful, intelligent voice. "It makes sense that if you were to combine two creatures into a hideous blend, the resulting monstrosity would be quite ill-tempered."

"Ferkle?" I asked, recognizing the voice. "Is that you?"

"Yes," came the reply. "Sadly, these resentful villains appear to be seeking revenge on me as well."

He then sat up, poking his head out of the bag.

Ferkle was the least idiotic village idiot in the kingdom.

In fact, he was quite intelligent, but he had gone into village idiocy because it was the family business. (Also, it was a lot easier than being a peasant, which was further proof of Ferkle's intellect.) Despite his smarts, he still had to *act* dumb to keep up appearances, for which reason he currently had a cucumber jammed in his ear.

"What did these scoundrels do to you?" Belinda asked him.

"Well, they *tried* to trick me into eating a poisoned apple," Ferkle replied. "And when I didn't fall for that, they tried to trick me with a poisoned pear, a poisoned banana, a poisoned mango, and a poisoned kumquat. After that, they just gave up and whacked me on the head with a club. Then they stuffed me in this sack, and the next thing I knew, I was here, listening to them blather on about their nefarious ⟨IQ BOOSTER!| plans."

"What does 'nefarious' mean?" Belinda asked, before I could explain it in a parenthetical comment.

"It means 'evil,'" Ferkle said, then glared at Ruprecht and Nerlim. "And your plan won't work!"

"How do you know?" Ruprecht asked. "I haven't even told you what the plan *is* yet."

"I already deduced what it is," Ferkle said. "It's—"

"Hey!" Ruprecht shouted. "I'm the revenge-seeking prince, so *I* get to reveal my evil plans, not you!" Then he looked at Belinda, Rover, and me and explained, "I had Princess Grace placed in the very center of the labyrinth.

So now you have a choice: You can try to rescue her—even though no human has ever emerged from the labyrinth alive. Or you can choose not to, but then everyone will know that you chickened out, and you will be detested throughout the kingdom for being cowardly, lily-livered, and erinaceous!" ⟨IQ BOOSTER!⟩

("Erinaceous" means "relating to the hedgehog." Really. While it is a decent insult, it is probable that Prince Ruprecht misused the word. He wasn't nearly as smart as Ferkle, and on our last adventure, I learned that sometimes, when he got riled up, he would often say the wrong thing.)

"With reputations like that, you will never be allowed to be knights again!" Ruprecht roared. "Instead, you will feel the shame and ridicule that *I* felt when you made me look bad by stealing my glory for rescuing Princess Grace!"

"But we *didn't* steal your glory," I reminded him. "We actually rescued Grace. So we deserved the glory, not you."

"I'm a prince!" Ruprecht snapped angrily. "Princes are the ones who are supposed to get the glory. Not peasants!" He said "peasants" with the same tone of disgust most people would have used for something they found stuck to the bottom of their shoe. "I'm under a tremendous amount of pressure to appear brave and valiant, while you were my lowly subjects! You were supposed to make me look good, but instead you made me look bad, so now I'm going to make you look bad too! Mwah-ha-ha-ha-ha!"

I glared at him, feeling all sorts of awful emotions.

I was angry at Prince Ruprecht for being a vengeful numbskull.

I was angry at Nerlim for concocting such an evil plan.

I was angry at myself for dropping my guard and allowing them to get the jump on us.

I was worried for the safety of Princess Grace.

And I was terrified, because I knew that I would soon be going into the labyrinth to save her.

CHAPTER FIVE

Why I Went into the Labyrinth

Even though the labyrinth was impossible to solve and filled with bloodthirsty minotaurs, I knew I would have to go into it.

This wasn't because, as Prince Ruprecht had said, I was worried about being known throughout the land as a lily-livered coward who somehow resembled a hedgehog.

It was for two other, more important reasons:

1) It was the right thing to do.

Even if I hadn't been a knight, it would have been wrong to leave Princess Grace—or anyone—in grave danger.

2) It was my fault she was in there.

If I hadn't nodded off on my sentry duty, then Princess Grace would never have been tricked by Nerlim into taking the poisoned apples. And since I had gotten Grace into this mess, then it was my responsibility to get her out. Although I was really hoping to keep the whole part about me screwing up a secret. Instead, I pretended that I was only going in because I was brave and honorable and courageous.

So I agreed to enter the labyrinth.

Then Ruprecht and Nerlim cut me loose, snickering

the entire time, and hurried off before any minotaurs wandered out of the labyrinth and devoured them.

They had also cut Belinda, Rover, and Ferkle free.

Belinda was going to join me in the labyrinth. But only for reason number one.

She hadn't screwed up and fallen asleep on the job. She was simply brave and honorable and courageous.

Rover was also going to join us in the labyrinth. But for a third reason: he was a fr-dog, and fr-dogs are loyal and true to their masters, and not really that smart.

And Ferkle was also going to join us in the labyrinth because . . .

"Actually," Ferkle said, "I'm not going in there."

"What?" I asked, surprised. "I thought you were part of our team!"

"I *am*," Ferkle insisted. "But there are many ways to be a part of a team. And the part I'm playing is: I'm the brains of this operation."

"But you have a cucumber in your ear," Belinda reminded him.

Ferkle sighed, took the cucumber out of his ear, and

tossed it into the bushes. "I have figured out something about this labyrinth. Prince Ruprecht said that no human has ever emerged from it alive. But that can't possibly be true."

"Why not?" Belinda asked.

"Well, someone built it, didn't they?" Ferkle replied. "And someone designed it. What happened to them?"

"Maybe the king of Extravagancia killed them all to keep the plans of the labyrinth a secret," I suggested.

"That seems a bit extreme," Ferkle said. "But also . . . Ruprecht said that Princess Grace had been placed in the very center of the labyrinth. Well, who placed her there? And how did *they* get out?"

"Hmmm," I said. "That's a good question."

"I *know*," Ferkle said. "And I'm going to get some answers. So while you look for Grace in the labyrinth, I'll do some research in town."

"Wait," I said. "Maybe all of us should do the research together. Since you're the village idiot, maybe no one will take you seriously."

"I'm not going to *tell* them I'm a village idiot," Ferkle

said dismissively. "And no one in Extravagancia knows me, so I'll be able to pose as a dignified gentleman from another kingdom and be treated with respect. Which reminds me, I should probably get rid of this." He pulled a live chicken out of his pants and tossed it into the bushes as well.

"We could help you," I said. "It sounds much safer than going through the labyrinth. . . ."

"It *is*," Ferkle agreed, "but you still need to go in. There's a chance I'm wrong. A very, very, very slim chance. But still, if we all go to town and then fail to find the information we need, we'll squander too much valuable time. Princess Grace is in very dire circumstances, thanks to the nitwit who allowed her to get poisoned by those apples."

"It doesn't really matter *who* allowed that to happen," I said quickly. "Although I'm sure that whoever did do it must feel really bad about the whole thing. The point is, Grace needs to be saved as fast as possible. So let's get to it!" I started for the mouth of the labyrinth.

"Sounds good," Ferkle said. "Although, before you go

running off into a dark and dangerous labyrinth, don't you think you ought to have some weapons? And torches? And twine?"

I paused, realizing that, once again, Ferkle was right.

Since Belinda and I had been captured at dinner, we didn't have any of our protective armor. Or any swords or knives or anything else that was sharp and pointy.

And it probably would have been helpful to have some light in the labyrinth so we could see.

And twine would have also been helpful to have in case we found a present for Princess Grace and wanted to put a nice bow on it.

Although it occurred to me that that probably wasn't why Ferkle had suggested bringing it.

"Er . . . why twine?" I asked.

"So you can find your way back out of the labyrinth," Ferkle explained. "You tie one end to a tree outside and unwind it as you go along. Then you can use it to retrace your steps to the exit after you locate the princess."

"Oh!" Belinda exclaimed. "That's really clever!"

"No kidding," Ferkle said. "Lucky for you, I happen

to have a ball of twine on me." Then he dug through his pockets, removing an assortment of vegetables, rocks, and startled-looking small rodents, until . . . "Aha! Here we are! Twine!"

"Thanks," I said, taking it from him. "I don't know what we would have done without you."

"You're about to find out," Ferkle said. "Because you're going in there without me."

Still, he stuck around to help us find some weapons and make some torches.

Sadly, there were no swords or knives lying about. And we didn't have the time to mine for ore, extract the precious metals, smelt them, and forge weapons. So we simply found a large stick that we could use as a club.

Then we found a slightly smaller stick and set it on fire to make a torch.

And then we tied one end of the twine to a tree.

And *then* we headed into the labyrinth.

"Good luck!" Ferkle yelled after us. "And remember, if you always go left, you'll be right!" With that, he ran off toward town.

"Bye!" Belinda and I yelled to him.

It was only *after* we entered the labyrinth that we realized we didn't have the slightest idea what his advice meant.

CHAPTER SIX

What the Labyrinth Was Like

You have probably encountered a maze before, quite likely on the children's menu at a restaurant. If so, I bet it looked something like this:

Can you unscramble these two-letter words?

FI

TI

OT

NI

That is *not* a labyrinth. A labyrinth is an enormous, twisty, confusing tangle of dank and drippy tunnels—and the dead ends are *literally* dead ends. If you go the wrong way, you'll fall into a bottomless pit, or be impaled by spears that shoot out of the walls, or get eaten by a minotaur.

I knew about all those dangers, because as we entered the cave, there was a nice little stand full of brochures with a cheerful sign saying TAKE ONE!

The brochure was a piece of parchment that looked like this:

WELCOME TO THE LABYRINTH OF EXTRAVAGANCIA, THE BIGGEST, TWISTIEST, MOST CONFOUNDING, MOST DANGEROUS LABYRINTH IN THE WORLD!

BE AWARE!

The Labyrinth is not recommended for small children, pregnant women, people with allergies to cattle, people who are allergic to poison, or people who are mortal.

The Labyrinth is an impossible-to-solve maze, stretching over a great distance, featuring too many tunnels to count, thousands of dead ends, and guaranteed hours of terror, horror, and dread.

You may encounter bottomless pits, razor-sharp spears, marauding zombies, vicious reptiles, falling rocks, boogeymen, imps, harpies, blugworts, snorklebarkers, crimson whingers, golden whizzbangs, off-white piddlebangers, grotesquerrels, gimmyjaws, stickypigs, wibblejibbles, velociraptors, chucklemucks, cave sharks, macksnatchers, smackwhackers, whackstackers, crackflackers, exploding numwraths, very large gerbils with horrible attitudes, assorted other things-that-go-bump-in-the-night, and of course . . .

The world-famous, exceptionally dangerous, extremely foul-tempered, bloodthirsty
MINOTAURS!!!

(All those who enter the Labyrinth hereby forfeit any claims against the Kingdom of Extravagancia for any wounding, mauling, impaling, crushing, or death suffered on the premises.)

Not surprisingly, after reading this, I began to feel a bit worried.

I turned back to the entrance, thinking that maybe we should duck out and offer to switch places with Ferkle, but a great portcullis suddenly dropped down, sealing off the exit and trapping us inside.

Now I felt even *more* worried.

Which only got worse a minute later when Belinda asked, "Do you know what Ferkle meant when he said 'If you always go left, you'll be right'?"

"Er . . . no," I admitted. "I was hoping *you* understood that."

Belinda shook her head sadly. "No. Why did that intelligent idiot have to be so cryptic? Why couldn't he have just said whatever he meant?"

"Maybe he thought he *wasn't* being cryptic," I said.

"Well, he was. How can we go left and right at the same time?"

I paused, thinking about this while I looked around in the gloom. We had quickly reached a junction where five different tunnels split off. The entrance to each looked exactly the same. If we hadn't been trailing twine behind us, I wouldn't have even remembered which tunnel we had just come from.

"If we go left, we can't go right," Belinda griped, frustrated. "Because we'll be going left."

"Wait a minute!" I exclaimed. "Ferkle didn't say 'If you always go left, you'll also go right.' He said, 'If you always go left, you'll *be* right.' Like he's using 'right' as a synonym for 'correct.'"

"So?" Belinda asked.

"Think about it: all these tunnels look exactly the same. If we don't have a system to keep track of the tunnels we've been through, we'll never remember which ones we've checked and which ones we haven't. But always going left *is* a system! If we always take the tunnel to the left at any junction, then we'll never get confused!"

Belinda screwed up her face. "Too late. I'm already confused."

"Then just look at this helpful illustration," I said.

"Oh!" Belinda exclaimed. "I get it now! Boy, it really helps to have a good illustrator!"

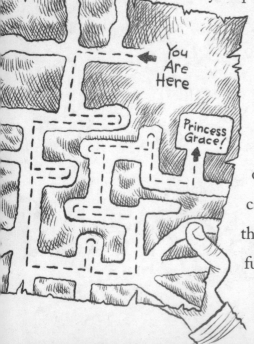

"It sure does," I agreed.

Using the advice Ferkle had given us, we promptly headed down the first tunnel to the left. We took our time, going slowly and cautiously, until we found that it dead-ended in a room full of vicious, bloodsucking cave lizards. We quickly knocked all of them senseless with our clubs, then retraced our steps to the junction (carefully rolling up the twine), and took the next tunnel to the left.

This tunnel led to a room full of freakishly large labyrinth beetles. Luckily, we had a freakishly large fr-dog with us, and he quickly ate them.

We retraced our steps to the junction once again, then took the *next* tunnel to the left. This one led to a small, unassuming pile of rubble.

"Hmmm," Belinda observed. "That's not really frightening or dangerous at all."

"There are going to be a lot of dead ends in this

labyrinth," I said. "I suppose they couldn't bring in something frightening or dangerous for all of them."

"I guess not," Belinda agreed. "Well, that's a relief."

"Yes," I said. "It sure is."

At which point the rubble tried to kill us.

CHAPTER SEVEN

How We—Wait a Second. Did You Just Say the *Rubble* Tried to Kill You???

Yes I did.

I know, I know. Usually rubble is only fragments of broken rock and stone and has no brain and therefore no ability to plot an attack, nor any muscles, legs, claws, or teeth to carry that attack out with.

But you're thinking of normal rubble.

This was cursed, homicidal rubble. Or "chrubble" for short.

It was rubble that had had a magical hex placed upon it to make it want to bludgeon people until they were dead.

Don't feel embarrassed if you've never heard of it. To

be honest, I had never heard of chrubble myself—until it tried to kill me.

Suddenly the pile of rocks came to life, forming itself into a humanoid shape with boulders for fists, like *this*:

And then it took a swing at me.

I ducked out of the way without a moment to spare as a boulder-fist sailed over my head and smashed into the wall.

The wall crumbled a bit where it had been struck, releasing a cascade of rubble to the floor. And then *that* rubble came to life, rolled across the floor, and joined the other rubble, making the chrubble humanoid form even bigger—and thus harder to escape.

Belinda had managed to get behind it and brought her club down on its head with all of her might.

Which did absolutely no good at all.

The club shattered into splinters while the chrubble didn't appear to have felt a thing.

Then it took a swing at Belinda, who barely managed to duck away. The boulder smashed into a wall, which created more rubble, which also joined the chrubble creature, making it even bigger.

"New plan!" Belinda announced. "Run!"

She bolted back down the tunnel. Rover and I followed right on her heels.

The chrubble came after us. With each thunderous step, the labyrinth shook. More rubble tumbled from the walls, which was then absorbed into the creature, which continued to swell in size. The bigger it got, the stronger it became, which meant it was able to create *more* rubble, which made it grow even bigger, which made it even stronger, which meant it could create even *more* rubble, which meant . . . Well, you get the idea.

If you have never been chased by an ever-growing creature made out of sentient rocks (and I'm guessing you haven't), consider yourself lucky. It was TERRIFYING.

"What do we do?" I screamed at Belinda as we ran. I didn't only scream because I was scared, but also because the sound of the chrubble coming after us was cacophonous. ◁ IQ BOOSTER!

("Cacophonous" means "really, really loud." Like a clap of thunder when you are right underneath it. Or the roar of a giant that has just dropped a house on his toe. The chrubble was so loud, it made my brain hurt.)

"I don't know!" Belinda screamed back. "I had the idea to run away! Now it's *your* turn to think of something!"

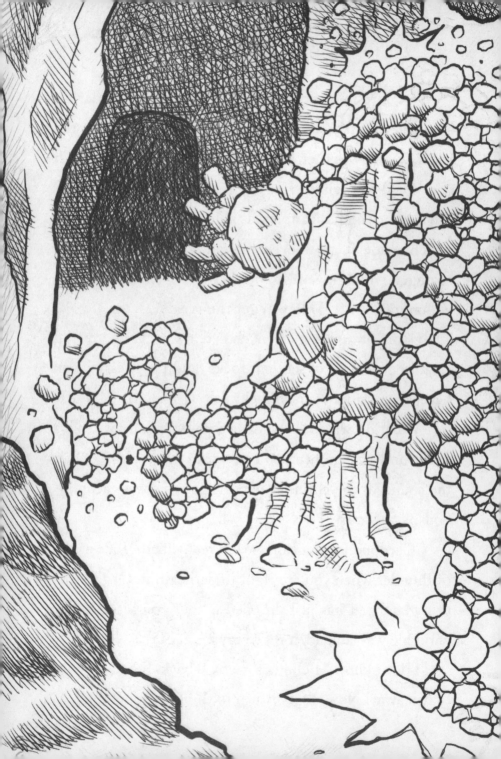

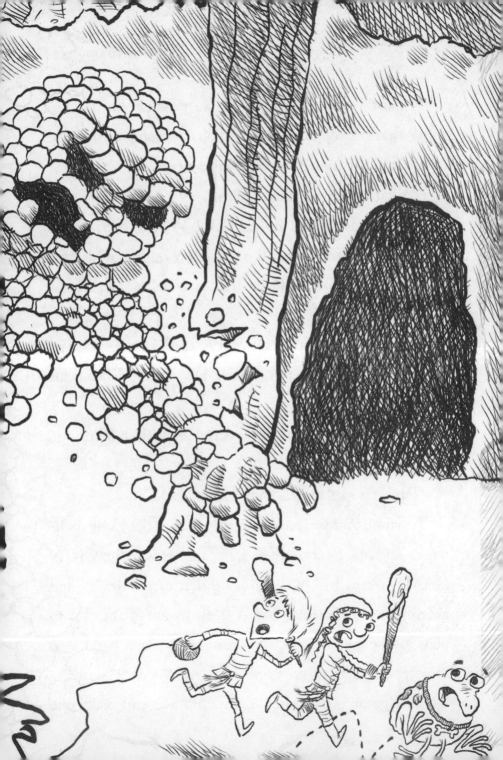

"I can't!" I yelled. "How can we possibly beat something that's made out of rock? You can't stab a rock! Or strangle it! Or trick it into drinking a poison!"

"What about smashing it?"

"That only makes more rocks! Which then try to smash *us*!" I leapt out of the way as a huge boulder-fist came crashing down where I had just been. "See what I mean?"

"Well, there must be some way to defeat this thing!" Belinda yelled. "Something must beat rock! What beats rock?"

The moment she put it that way, I had a flash of insight. I actually knew the answer.

"Paper!" I exclaimed. "Paper beats rock!"

I assume that you have probably played the game rock-paper-scissors. I certainly had, because it was the ONLY GAME we had in olden times. Dice, cards, timers, and video game consoles all hadn't been invented yet. But to play rock-paper-scissors all you needed was a hand, and most people had at least one of those. So we played it a lot. The game is very simple. You and a friend make one of three symbols with your hands at the same time: a fist represents rock, an open palm represents paper, and two fingers represent scissors. Rock beats scissors, scissors beat paper . . . and PAPER BEATS ROCK.

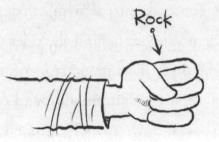

Rock

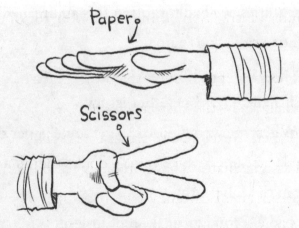

Paper

Scissors

Now, if you're like me, at some point in your life, you have probably thought, *This makes no sense at all. I mean, obviously rock beats scissors, because you can smash a pair of scissors with a rock. And scissors beat paper, because you can cut paper with scissors. But how on earth does paper beat rock?*

To which some smarty-pants might reply, *Well, paper wraps rock.* Which, let's face it, is a lame answer. Wrapping something isn't beating it. It's just making that object cozy.

So in that moment it occurred to me that perhaps there was some ancient wisdom behind the rules of rock-paper-scissors. Maybe some distant ancestors of ours had recognized this was important information and come up with a clever way to pass it down to us, but somehow, over the centuries, we had forgotten this and turned the warning into a ridiculous game.

Not that I had any time to explain this.

Plus, there was one other issue:

"Where are we supposed to get some paper right now?" Belinda screamed as we ran. "I doubt there's a stationery store in this labyrinth!"

I had a second great flash of insight.

"The welcome brochure!" I exclaimed. "I still have it!"

With that, I whipped out the brochure I had grabbed at the entrance of the labyrinth and raised it high over my head.

The chrubble instantly stopped chasing us. All the rocks in its body grated on one another at once, in what sounded like a shriek of fear.

I spun around, holding the brochure in front of me as menacingly as I could.

This was not very menacing at all, really. But it appeared to terrify the chrubble.

It recoiled from me, trembling like it was experiencing an earthquake. Every rock in its body vibrated against all the other rocks, making it sound like a giant maraca.

"Not so tough now, are you?" I asked

The chrubble made a pitiful squeak and backed away.

I swatted it with the brochure.

The creature immediately fell apart. In an instant, it was just a pile of normal rubble again.

Belinda turned to me, impressed. "I can't believe that actually worked. Good thinking, Tim."

"Thanks." I carefully tucked the brochure back into my pants, just in case we would need it later.

Belinda picked up a good-sized piece of rubble and carried it with her as we continued onward.

"What's that for?" I asked.

"In case we run into any giant scissors. Then we can smash them."

"Giant scissors?" I scoffed. "That's the most ridiculous thing I've ever heard."

Of course, that's exactly what we ran into in the next tunnel.

How We Defeated the Giant Scissors of Doom

It actually wasn't that hard.

CHAPTER EIGHT

What Really Frightened Me in the Labyrinth

We went on like that for a while.

We would follow a tunnel, end up in a dead end with some vicious beast or life-threatening obstacle, escape at the last second, then retrace our steps and try another tunnel, which would inevitably also turn out to be a dead end harboring yet another vicious beast or life-threatening obstacle.

Occasionally, to mix things up, we had to get past a life-threatening obstacle that was *filled* with vicious beasts. Like when we came to the Chasm of the Cave Sharks.

This one wasn't a dead end. It was smack-dab in the middle of the route through the labyrinth, so we had to get past it.

However, it was a formidable ◁ IQ BOOSTER! barrier. ("Formidable" means "inspiring fear through being impressively large or intense." As in: "Convincing your parents to let you stay up past your bedtime to read this book might be a formidable challenge, but I'm sure you can rise to it.")

"Think we could jump across it?" Belinda asked.

"I think we could jump *halfway* across it," I replied. "And then we would plummet down into the bottom of the chasm and get eaten alive."

Belinda peered at the sharks circling beneath us. "Do you suppose there's a chance that they *wouldn't* eat us? Maybe they're vegetarians."

"I don't think there's any such thing as vegetarian sharks," I told her.

At that very moment a disturbingly large cockroach happened to blunder over the edge of the chasm. It tumbled all the way down, plopped into the water—and was immediately devoured by a dozen sharks at once.

"You're right," Belinda agreed. "Those sharks are hungry enough to eat *anything*. We're going to have to find something we can use to get across."

We started poking around in the darker recesses of the labyrinth for anything useful, like a rope we could swing across on, or a pole we could vault over with—or possibly even a nice sturdy bridge and a large supply of shark repellent. But all I could find were disgusting things like cave worms, spiders, and vampire bats.

"What kind of evil weirdo designed this labyrinth?" I muttered angrily. "I mean, who says, 'Gee, this steep, deadly chasm isn't really dangerous enough—we should put some man-eating sharks at the bottom of it'?"

"You know who you should *really* be angry at?" Belinda asked. "The person who got us into this mess."

"You mean Prince Ruprecht?" I asked. "Because he forced us to come into this labyrinth to rescue Princess Grace?"

"No. Not him."

"Nerlim? Because he came up with this dastardly plan—and gave the poisoned apples to Grace?"

"No. Not him, either."

"Princess Grace then? Because she was so easily tricked into taking the poisoned apples?"

"No. Not her."

I grew uneasy, not liking where this conversation was going. "Then who?"

"Whoever fell asleep while protecting the castle gates in the first place. It was *his* job to make sure something like this didn't happen."

I grimaced. Luckily, it was dark in the cave, and I was quite far away from Belinda, so she couldn't see my reaction.

I knew that the right thing to do was to own up to my mistake, but I was afraid to. Because I didn't want Belinda to know the truth. My failure had ultimately led to the predicament we were in, and it made sense that she would hate me if she knew the truth.

So instead of being honest, I said, "I'm pretty sure it was Sir Cumference who fell asleep. He's always nodding off."

"Really?" Belinda asked, growing upset. "That guy is always complaining that we're not working hard enough—and then he's sleeping on the job? We should tell Sir Vyval about this when we get back."

I gulped, knowing this would only make things worse. "Er . . . maybe we shouldn't do that."

"Why not?"

"I just don't like the idea of tattling on other people. I mean, what if Sir Cumference found out that you're actually a girl? Would you want him telling Sir Vyval that?"

"Of course not! But this is different. I haven't

endangered anyone's life. Sir Cumference has. If he fell asleep on duty, then Sir Vyval should know about it. Any knight who makes that big of a mistake ought to be punished for it. Maybe they should even be kicked out of the Knight Brigade."

"Urk," I said. Partly because I was worried about what Belinda was saying. And partly because I had come across what I thought was a piece of rope, only to find that it was a big, slimy cave worm.

"You agree with me about this, don't you?" Belinda asked.

"Um . . . ," I said, trying to

avoid answering. I was certainly in favor of Sir Cumference getting kicked out of the Knight Brigade if he made a mistake. Sir Cumference was mean and rude, and he often stole my dessert. Especially on pudding night. But it was a very different story when *I* was the one who had made the mistake.

The cave worm tried to sink its fangs into me.

(I know worms usually don't have fangs. But sharks don't usually live in caves either. This labyrinth was full of surprises.)

I quickly tossed the worm aside. The moment Rover saw it, he shot out his tongue, snapped up the worm, and gulped it down.

"That wasn't an answer," Belinda said, sounding a tiny bit suspicious. "Do you agree with me or not?"

Once again I didn't answer her. But this time it wasn't because I was trying to avoid answering the question. Well, okay, it was *partly* because I didn't want to answer the question. But mostly it was because I had just had an idea.

"I think I know how to get across the chasm," I said.

CHAPTER NINE

How We Got Past the Cave Sharks

If you have a dog, you probably know that there is a magical spot on every dog's belly. When you scratch your dog in just the right place, their hind leg jiggles around like crazy.

Well, there is a magical spot like that on a fr-dog, too. Only, when you scratch him there, his tongue fires out.

So I picked up Rover, aimed him carefully toward the exact spot I needed on the ceiling of the labyrinth, and then scratched his spot.

Sure enough, his big, sticky tongue fired out and stuck to a stalactite. ◁ IQ BOOSTER!

(A stalactite is a conelike structure that dangles from the roof of a cave. It looks kind of like an icicle, except that icicles are made of ice and stalactites are made of rock. These are not to be confused with stalagmites, which are cones that point up toward the roof of the cave. You can remember the difference like this: stalactites have to hold *tight* to the roof of the cave so they don't fall off, while stalagmites *might* reach the ceiling of the cave someday. Now you have learned some cool new words *and* some geology. Your parents are going to be very impressed.)

Once I was sure that Rover's tongue had a nice, firm grip on the stalactite, I clutched him tightly and swung across the chasm like this:

Far below us, the cave sharks thrashed about and snapped their teeth hungrily, but it didn't do them one bit of good, because Rover and I made it across the chasm safely.

WARNING! DO NOT ATTEMPT THIS WITH A NORMAL FROG.

While normal frogs *do* have sticky tongues, they are not nearly sticky enough or strong enough to support your weight should you need to swing over a chasm full of ravenous, man-eating cave sharks. Fr-dogs have unusually strong and sticky tongues, and even then, I wouldn't recommend using one to swing over a chasm full of ravenous, man-eating cave sharks unless it was an absolute emergency. This is not the sort of thing you should be doing to pass the time. If you have a choice, why not play a nice game of checkers instead?

"Great idea, Tim!" Belinda exclaimed when she saw what I had done.

"Thanks!" I said. "Heads up!" I swung Rover back across the chasm, and then Belinda grabbed on to him and started back over herself.

Unfortunately, fr-dog tongues aren't quite as well designed for swinging over chasms of deadly sharks as, say, a rope might be. Belinda had almost—but not quite—reached my side when Rover's tongue suddenly came free.

"Tiiiiiiiiiiiiiiimmmmmmmmmmm!!!!!!!" Belinda shouted as she and Rover suddenly fell.

Which forced me to do this:

After that, Belinda and I both had to sit for a while to rest. Our hearts were thudding in our chests.

Although there *was* one positive result of this (besides the fact that Belinda and Rover weren't eaten alive): in all the excitement of nearly dying, Belinda seemed to have forgotten about getting Sir Cumference in trouble.

"Whew," she said. "That was too close for comfort. If it wasn't for you, we'd have been shark chow."

"Are you okay?" I asked.

"I'm a little shaken, but I'll be all right. Do you think Rover's okay?"

I looked at my fr-dog. His tongue seemed a little more stretched out than usual, but otherwise he appeared to be fine.

"I *think* so," I said. "I wonder what he's thinking."

"I guess we'll never know," said Belinda.

CHAPTER NINE AND A HALF

What Rover Was Thinking

Dum de dum de dum de doo. Doo be doo be doo. Dum dum dum dum. Doo be doo. Dum de dum de dum de doo. Doo be doo be doo. Dum dum dum dum. Doo be doo. Dum de dum de dum de doo. Doo be doo be doo. Dum dum dum dum. Doo be doo. Dum de dum de dum de doo. Doo be doo be doo. Dum dum dum dum. Doo be doo.

FOOD! Dum de dum de dum de doo. Doo be doo be doo. Dum dum dum dum. Doo be doo. Dum de dum de dum de doo. Doo be doo be doo. Dum dum dum dum. Doo be doo.

Dum de dum de dum de doo. Doo be doo

be doo. Dum dum dum dum. Doo be doo. Dum de dum de dum de doo. Doo be doo be doo. Dum dum dum dum. Doo be doo. Dum de dum de dum de doo. Doo be doo be doo. Dum dum dum dum. Doo be doo. FOOD! Yum yum yum! Dum de dum de dum de doo. Doo be doo be doo. Dum dum dum dum. Doo be doo. Dum de dum de dum de doo. Doo be doo be doo. Dum dum dum dum. Doo be doo. Dum de dum de dum de doo. Doo be doo be doo. Dum dum dum dum. Doo be doo. Dum de dum de dum de doo. Doo be doo be doo. Dum dum dum du—

SQUIRRELS!!!! I HATE YOU!!!! YOU'RE THE SCUM OF THE EARTH!!! DIE, STUPID SQUIRRELS!!!! DIE!!!!!!!

CHAPTER TEN

What Further Horrors We Faced

As you can probably tell from Rover's furious barking, we had come across some squirrels.

There were plenty of horrible, terrifying creatures on earth: dragons, chimeras, sphinxes, blugworts, and sea serpents, to name a few.

Rover didn't care about any of them. But he *hated* squirrels.

I have no idea what squirrels had ever done to him, but any time he saw one, he would go after it with a white-hot fury.

As it happened, the squirrels we had come across in the labyrinth weren't normal squirrels at all. They were exceptionally grotesque ⟨IQ BOOSTER!⟩ squirrels.

("Grotesque" means "comically or repulsively ugly." I could use it in a sentence to explain it, but I think that, in this case, an illustration would work much better. Here are some grotesque squirrels:)

These grotesque squirrels, or "grotesquerrels" for short, were known for having grotesque behavior in addition to their grotesque looks. While regular squirrels hoarded nuts for the winter, grotesquerrels attacked people with them, pelting unsuspecting peasants with acorns and the like. (My cousin Gerald had once nearly lost an eye in a hail of almonds.) Grotesquerrels also bit, scratched, and tried to urinate on you as you walked under their trees.

Thanks to Rover, these grotesquerrels never got the chance. We came across a small mob of them, which had certainly been plotting to do some dastardly thing to us, but the moment Rover saw them, he went wild, barking and snarling, which scared the pants off the mean little critters. They scattered in fear as my fr-dog bore down on them.

So, for once, we managed to get through an obstacle without too much trouble.

In fact, we had a brief run of good luck.

The blugwort we encountered was sound asleep.

The gimmyjaws we ran into had just eaten a chuckle-muck, so they were in no mood to chase us down.

Which also took care of the chucklemuck.

The crimson whinger had left a note on the entrance of its lair:

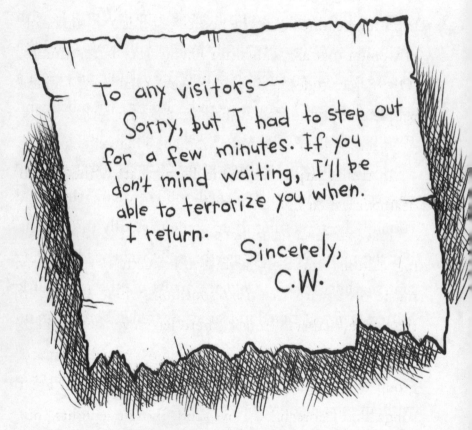

To any visitors —
    Sorry, but I had to step out for a few minutes. If you don't mind waiting, I'll be able to terrorize you when I return.
            Sincerely,
            C.W.

We chose not to wait.

And the exploding numwrath appeared to have exploded prematurely shortly before we showed up.

So that was all well and good.

We weren't nearly as lucky with the harpies, though.

Harpies are one of the most terrifying beasts of all time.

I know that a lot of people will tell you harpies are frightful creatures with the bodies of birds and the heads of women that are known for having very foul attitudes. (Or fowl attitudes, really, since they're half-bird.) These people do not know what they are talking about.

A bird with the head of a woman? That's ridiculous.

In truth, harpies are living harps that soothe you to death with their music.

Have you ever heard harp music? It is the most relaxing, calming music on earth. You honestly can't play any music on a harp that *isn't* soothing, which is why, in the entire history of music, there has never been a harp solo on any major dance hit. (The most popular musical group in my time, the Pied Pipers, not only had great songs like "Leprechaun Love" and "Boogie Knights," but also would drive all the rats out of your town.)

The music of the harpy was dangerously peaceful and relaxing. It lulled people into thinking pleasant, happy thoughts until they became so tranquil and relaxed that they fell into an eternal sleep.

So naturally, we were terrified to run into them . . .

Until they started playing their music.

Almost instantly we started to feel fine.

"Harpies!" Belinda yelled when she first saw them. "Look out! We need to escape . . . from the stress of our usual lives . . . and maybe hang out here for a century or two." The fear vanished from her face and was replaced with what looked frighteningly close to delight.

The despicable harpies had cruelly filled their lair with extremely comfortable-looking furniture. Belinda started for a pile of dangerously plush cushions.

"No!" I screamed. Or at least I *tried* to scream. It came out in a far more quiet and conversational tone than I had intended. "Don't listen to the music. Put your fingers in your ears."

I could already feel the horridly delightful music working on me. I felt frighteningly calm and serene. My arms wanted to hang limply by my sides for the rest of my life. But I forced them up and jammed my fingers in my ears.

Instantly the music faded. I stopped feeling happy and relaxed and began to feel appropriately upset and frightened again.

Belinda managed to plug her ears at the last second. With relief, I saw her go from calm to freaked out.

"We need to get out of here!" I shouted.

"What?" Belinda replied. "I can't hear you! I have my fingers in my ears!"

Or it was something like that. I couldn't really tell for sure because I had my fingers in my ears.

So I tried to show her what to do. I attempted to run for the door.

But the harpies had already moved into our path. They strummed their strings even louder and more pleasantly. Even though I had my fingers firmly lodged in my ears, the music began to leak into my head.

I stopped being frightened and started to become dangerously blissful. I found myself being drawn to an exceptionally cozy-looking armchair, where I could sit down and relax for the next few years....

Thankfully, Belinda came to my rescue. She raced toward the harpies....

Well, really, she kind of casually sauntered over to them. And then she kicked one in the strings.

The strings snapped, making a sharp, atonal noise that completely ruined the wickedly lovely song that the harpy had been playing.

That was all it took to break the spell. I was immediately agitated again.

The harpy with the broken strings snarled angrily in the most melodious and delightful fashion while the remaining harpies played even more pleasant music.

But I had a few seconds before I succumbed. **IQ BOOSTER!**

(To "succumb" means "to yield or give in to." As in: "The snooty parent originally thought the book wasn't good enough for their child, but after reading a few hilarious—and yet educational—pages, they succumbed to its charms.")

I snatched up one of the comfy pillows and flung it at the harpies.

I know a pillow isn't really much of a weapon, but harpies (and harps) are famously top-heavy and therefore quite easy to tip over.

The pillow struck the first harpy in a dainty yet effective manner. The harpy wobbled and then toppled, banging into the next harpy, which fell over into the next harpy . . . and so on. They all went down like a line of dominoes.

Several more of the harpies' strings snapped. The nightmarishly lovely music stopped playing.

Belinda and I took advantage of the intermission and fled as fast as we could. Keeping our fingers stuck in our ears, just in case the harpies managed an encore, we raced down the tunnel into the deeper reaches of the labyrinth, until we were far, far away from the awful, terrible, incredibly relaxing music.

At which point we discovered that we were hopelessly lost.

CHAPTER ELEVEN

Why We Got Angry

Belinda and I didn't realize we were lost right away. It happened like this:

"Whew," I said. "That was another close call. Good work back there."

"What?" Belinda asked. She still had her fingers jammed in her ears for protection.

I pulled her fingers out for her. "It's safe now. I was just saying good work back there, fighting those harpies."

"You too. We make a good team."

"A *great* team."

"An *amazing* team."

"A *fantastic* team. Now, where's the twine you've been carrying?"

Belinda suddenly grew upset. "Me?! I thought *you* were carrying the twine!"

And of course I grew upset too. "I thought *you* were carrying it!"

At which point we instantly stopped being a great, amazing, and fantastic team.

We became a lousy, angry, poorly functioning team instead.

To be honest, I couldn't remember *who* was supposed to have been holding the twine—or if we had ever discussed this. I couldn't even remember the last time I had *seen* the twine. (If I'd had this book, I could have gone back through the illustrations to see where we had stopped carrying it, and therefore figure out who had dropped it, but that wasn't the case.)

So maybe I was the one who had dropped it. But it could have just as easily been Belinda. And I was already feeling ashamed about having fallen asleep on the job back at the castle and getting us into this mess, so I certainly didn't want to be blamed for yet another screwup.

Plus, both of us were exhausted and on edge after so

many ordeals. You know how people get cranky when they get tired? (Even adults?) Well, imagine how cranky you would be if you were tired and scared and worried that the next time you rounded a corner, you'd come across something with sharp teeth and claws that wanted to disembowel ⟨ IQ BOOSTER! ⟩ you.

("Disembowel" means "to remove the innards from," your innards being all the stuff like your intestines and your stomach and your spleen that, despite being gooey and disgusting, are very important to keep *inside* your body. Disemboweling is a really terrible way to die, and the fact that we even have a word for it tells you that it was a disturbingly common occurrence back in my day.)

Anyhow, given the stress that Belinda and I were under, we ended up like *this*:

"How could you lose the twine?" I shouted. "We needed that to survive!"

"I didn't lose it!" Belinda shouted back. "*You* did, you nitwit!"

"You're the nitwit!"

"Pinhead!"

"Idiot!"

"Numbskull!"

"Noodlebrain!"

It went on like that for a while, until we ran out of insults to call each other. Then we declared that we weren't friends anymore and were no longer on speaking terms.

At which point things became very awkward.

If we had fought like this back in our village, we would have each stormed home and been able to cool off.

But we couldn't really storm off to different parts of the labyrinth, because even though we were upset with one another, we knew that splitting up would be incredibly dumb. Our chances of surviving and finding our way back out again were already very slim, given that one of us had lost the twine.[1] So we had to stay

---

1. I'm still pretty sure it was Belinda.

together, even though we were livid at each other.

And because we were lost in a labyrinth, we really needed to communicate. It would have been very helpful to say things like *Do you think we should go left or right here? Or I'd say left, because the right tunnel smells very dragon-y. Or I'm sorry I got upset with you. I'm very stressed out. You're my best friend, and I think we should start talking again.*

But we were too stubborn to say anything like that. Instead, we kept giving each other angry glares, which were very hard to understand. Belinda's glares could have meant all sorts of things like, *I'm still angry at you for calling me a noodlebrain. Or It's the right tunnel that smells dragon-y, you dingbat, not the left one. Or There's no way we're ever getting out of here, and it's all your fault.*"

Although, after a while of silently bumbling through the labyrinth, Belinda gave me a very different kind of look. Like this:

I wasn't sure what to make of this at first, but then I figured out that it meant "Oh no! There's a minotaur in the labyrinth ahead of us!"

Because there was a minotaur in the labyrinth ahead of us.

CHAPTER TWELVE

Aaaaaaaaah!!!!!
A Minotaur!!!!!!

✄ ▭▭▭▭▭ ✄

My first reaction upon seeing the minotaur was terror. Although really, my first reaction upon running into *anything* in a dark, spooky labyrinth would have been terror. Even a kitten holding a bouquet of roses would have been terrifying to stumble across down there.

My second reaction was confusion.

I assume that you have seen pictures of minotaurs. And they probably all looked like *this*:

In fact, if you want to go do an internet search for minotaur images, I'm sure you'll find a few hundred that look like that. (I can wait a bit if you want to do this.)

Back in my day, we didn't have the internet, but I had still seen a good three or four drawings of minotaurs, and that's what they all looked like. And I had heard many tales of minotaurs, and they were always described as having the head of a bull and the body of a man.

But the one we were facing looked like this:

"Hey there!" the creature said cheerfully. "How's it going?"

"Uh . . . ," Belinda said, obviously as surprised as I was. "Not so great. Pardon me for asking, but . . . are you a minotaur?"

"That's right!" the minotaur replied. "I'm part man and part bull, so what else would I be? My name's Chad. It's nice to meet you."

"Um . . . ," I said. "No offense, but . . . I've always heard that minotaurs have the head of a bull and the body of a man."

"Really?" Chad asked, sounding genuinely surprised. "Do you also think that centaurs have the head of a horse and the body of a man?"

"Er . . . no," I said.

"But you think that minotaurs have bull heads and human bodies? That's weird." Chad rolled his eyes, which made him look even more ridiculous. "Minotaurs are simply part man and part bull. It doesn't really matter which parts are which. Like, my sister has the arms and legs of a woman but the body and head of a bull. And my brother has the front of a bull and the rear of a bull, and the midriff of a human. And my cousin Hubert has the head of a human and the body of an armadillo."

"An armadillo?" Belinda asked, surprised. "That's not part bull at all."

"I know," Chad admitted. "Hubert's adopted."

Cousin Hubert

Aunt Eunice

I have to admit, I was not only thrown by Chad's appearance, but also by his pleasant attitude. Everything else we had encountered in the labyrinth had been malicious and determined to kill us. Even the rubble. But now, the creature we had been warned about the most was ... friendly.

I wondered if it was all some sort of devious trick.

"Are you planning to eat us?" I asked.

"Eat you?" Chad repeated, and then burst into laughter. "Why would a minotaur want to eat a human? Bulls are vegetarians!"

"That's what I said!" Belinda exclaimed, then looked to me. "Remember when I said that? Back before we even came in here? I said that bloodthirsty minotaurs don't make any sense!"

"You can say that again!" Chad chuckled good-naturedly. "Say, why *did* you guys even come in here? This place is dangerous!"

"We didn't *want* to come in," I explained. "But our friend, Princess Grace, is being held captive in the very center of the labyrinth, and we're trying to rescue her. We're knights."

"Really?" Chad gave us a skeptical look. "You don't look like knights to me."

And you don't look like a minotaur, I thought, but I didn't say it.

Belinda asked, "I don't suppose you know how to get to the center of this labyrinth?"

"Of course I do!" Chad replied joyfully. "You've actually managed to get pretty close. I'd be happy to show you the rest of the way!"

"That'd be great!" I said.

"Just follow me!" Chad trotted off into the labyrinth.

Belinda, Rover, and I dropped in behind him.

As it turned out, Chad wasn't merely friendly; he was desperate to make friends. Which made sense, given that the other creatures we had run into hadn't seemed remotely friendly at all. Chad was also a bit of a chatterbox.

"It's nice to meet some friendly people down here for once," he said, taking care to lead us on a route that didn't pass through any life-threatening obstacles. "Or, at least, some friendly people who are still alive. I mean, I've found the remains of quite a few people who I assume were friendly, before they got killed. And it's hard to make friends with anything that lives down here, because, well . . . I'm gonna just say it. Most of them aren't very nice. Did you, by any chance, run into the very large gerbils with horrible attitudes?"

"No," I said.

"Well, consider yourself lucky. Those guys are the *worst*. So insulting! And don't even get me started on the bandersnatch. She's a real piece of work."

It went on like that for a while. Chad led us through the labyrinth, sharing all sorts of gossip about which inhabitants were mean and which were unsanitary and which ones would try to decapitate you and then eat your innards. It sounded awful. I kept trying to ask Chad what he was even doing living in there, but I couldn't get a word in edgewise. Eventually we arrived at a scary-looking door that had several locks holding it shut.

"Here we are!" Chad announced. "The dead center of the labyrinth. You'll have to undo all those latches and locks, though. I can't be of any more service here." He held up a foreleg. "See? No opposable thumbs. Just hooves. Which makes drinking a cup of tea a real chore."

Belinda and I stepped up to the door. It had a menacing look to it, as though it was designed to keep something extremely dangerous and scary from getting out.

We slowly began to undo all the locks and latches, which clanked and groaned ominously. Finally, the last one gave way and the door swung open, its hinges screeching like angry banshees. A gust of stale air rushed out of the mysterious room.

Cautiously we peered through the doorway to find . . .

Princess Grace.

Which filled me with joy and relief.

Although she was surrounded by cave snakes.

Which made all that joy and relief vanish in an instant.

CHAPTER THIRTEEN

What Went Wrong Next

The center of the labyrinth, where Grace was being held prisoner, was surprisingly well decorated, given that it was in the Labyrinth of Doom. Normally, it looked like this:

See? There were comfortable chairs and a bed and some oil lamps and a nice pot of daisies. Sure, it was a bit dank and musty, but compared to the rest of the labyrinth, it was awfully nice.

But at the moment it looked like *this*:

Dozens of venomous  cave snakes had breached the walls and were closing in on the princess. We had arrived just in time to help her fight them off.

(You probably think you know what "venomous" means. But you should be aware, there is actually a difference between "venomous" and "poisonous." Something that is poisonous is dangerous to *eat*, either killing you—or, in our case, making you pass out so that the bad guys can capture you and force you into a labyrinth. Whereas venomous things harm you by biting you—or stinging you—and injecting venom. Venomous plants and animals include cave snakes, boomslangs, basilisks, and the supremely dangerous deathnettle, which has a venom so toxic that merely brushing against it will make you explode.)

Anyhow, within a few seconds of our arrival, the central chamber of the labyrinth looked like *this*:

We grabbed whatever we could and attacked the cave snakes. I grabbed a nice chair. Belinda grabbed an expensive-looking end table. Grace grabbed a fancy lamp.

Chad didn't grab anything because, as you know, he had no opposable thumbs. Only hooves. He did try to stomp on some of the cave snakes—although he quickly became distracted by the daisies.

The cave snakes obviously weren't expecting to be assaulted with exquisite home furnishings. Or hooves. They quickly retreated back through the holes in the walls and slithered off into the labyrinth.

Princess Grace now had time to greet us properly. "Tim!" she exclaimed, giving me a hug. "And Bull! It's so good to see you!"

(Remember, she thought Belinda was a boy named Bull.)

"Er . . . actually, I'm only *half*-bull," Chad said, looking a bit offended. "And I have a name. It's Chad."

"I was talking to my friend here," Grace told him. "But it's very nice to make your acquaintance too!" She then looked to us. "I hope you haven't had too much trouble coming to rescue me."

"To be honest, we did," Belinda said. "It was quite an ordeal."

"Oh fiddlesticks!" Grace cursed. "I really tried to rescue myself this time. But that door was locked fast from the other side. I'm so sorry that I put you through all this! I should have never accepted those apples from that weird woman who came to the castle—"

This started to make me feel guilty again, so I quickly cut her off. "It wasn't your fault," I said. "It was . . ."

I was going to say *my fault*, but I hesitated, because I was still afraid to admit it.

"It was the fault of Sir Cumference," Belinda said before I could work up the nerve to admit the truth.

"Ooh!" Princes Grace said, steaming. "I'm going to have that guy kicked out of the Knight Brigade the moment we get back to the castle!"

"Oh," I said weakly, feeling even worse. "Well, actually . . ."

"And speaking of getting back to the castle," Grace went on, "I'm done with this labyrinth. How do we get out of here?"

Belinda and I both looked to Chad expectantly.

Chad didn't say anything. He was chewing on the daisies with ecstasy. "Oooh," he said to himself. "Mmmm . . . these are amazing. Light and crisp with just a hint of pollen . . ." He suddenly paused in mid-chew and asked, "Why are you all staring at me?"

"We're waiting for you to tell us how we get out of here," I said.

"Why do you think that *I* would know that?" Chad asked.

"Because you're the minotaur!" I exclaimed. "You knew how to get us to the center of the labyrinth!"

"Well, yes," Chad said. "I did."

"And you don't know how to get us back out again?" I asked.

"No," Chad said, like I was the village idiot. "If I knew how to get out of the labyrinth, why would I still be *in* the labyrinth? The labyrinth is horrible! It's full of monsters and deadly obstacles and very large gerbils with horrible attitudes. Plus, it's almost impossible to get a decent meal inside here! Do you know how long it's been since I've had daisies like this? Or any flowers at all? I mostly subsist on labyrinth fungus, which tastes awful."

"How long have you been in here?" Belinda asked.

"For as long as I can remember," Chad said. "Ever since I was half-calf, half-baby. Just a little minotaur. Or, as I like to think of it, a mini-taur." He chuckled at his own joke.

I didn't laugh, though. Any excitement I had felt upon rescuing Princess Grace was quickly giving way to panic. "So . . . you don't know the way out. And Bull lost the twine that would have led us back to the entrance. . . ."

"I didn't lose it!" Belinda snapped. "*You* did!"

"It doesn't matter *who* lost it,"[2] I said. "What matters is that we're trapped inside this labyrinth! If Chad hasn't been able to find his way out over all this time, then the chances of *us* finding our way back out are nonexistent! We're going to be stuck in here for the rest of our lives— which probably won't be very long, given all the bloodthirsty monsters and deadly obstacles!"

"Boy oh boy," Princess Grace said, "that is a very negative attitude."

"Of course it is!" I exploded. "Because there is nothing to be positive about! We are in extreme danger here! Things are as bad as they could possibly be!"

NOTE TO READERS:

You might think, like Princess Grace, that I was sounding really whiny and overreacting here. But the fact is that our situation was really, really horrible. I even have

---

2. I *really* think it was Belinda.

proof. Queen Beatrice of Brilliantia, who was regarded as the smartest person in all the kingdoms, once devised a Scale of Despair, which I will show you right now.

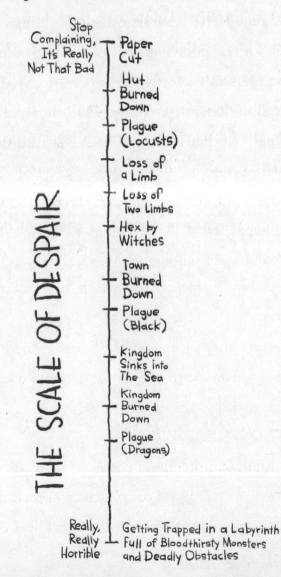

THE SCALE OF DESPAIR

Stop Complaining, It's Really Not That Bad — Paper Cut

Hut Burned Down

Plague (Locusts)

Loss of a Limb

Loss of Two Limbs

Hex by Witches

Town Burned Down

Plague (Black)

Kingdom Sinks into The Sea

Kingdom Burned Down

Plague (Dragons)

Really, Really Horrible — Getting Trapped in a Labyrinth Full of Bloodthirsty Monsters and Deadly Obstacles

See? I wasn't overreacting at all.

If anything, I was *under*reacting. I was only throwing a small tantrum. I should have been completely freaking out.

And I *might* have done that. I was building up to it . . .

When a secret door suddenly popped open in the wall.

It was built so perfectly that none of us had had the slightest idea that it was there. One moment the wall looked totally normal and, well, wall-ish. And the next, it was actually a door.

And then the most incredible, amazing thing I had ever seen happened.

Ferkle entered the room.

CHAPTER FOURTEEN

How to Get Out of a Labyrinth

Of course we were all flabbergasted. ⟨IQ BOOSTER!⟩

("Flabbergasted" means "completely astonished or confounded." It's how you might feel if you suddenly discovered that the earth actually orbits around the sun. Or that your best friend is really three leprechauns standing on one another's shoulders in a realistic human costume—which you might not think is very likely, but which was surprisingly common in olden times.)

"Hey, guys," Ferkle said casually. He glanced at Chad. "I see you met a minotaur."

The rest of us were all so stunned, we could barely get words out.

"H-h-how did you—" Princess Grace began.

"Wh-wh-where did you—" Belinda stammered.

"Wh-wh-what the—" I said.

"Ribbit," said Rover.

"I did exactly what we discussed," Ferkle said to Belinda and me. "I went to find the guy who had designed the labyrinth and placed Grace inside it. It took me a while, because he had built a maze around his home."

"Like a labyrinth full of bloodthirsty beasts and deadly obstacles?" Belinda asked.

"Er . . . no," Ferkle said. "It was a hedge maze. But it was rather complex, and the hedges had prickles. I got scratched a few times. It was quite an ordeal." He pointed to his elbow, where there was a scratch so thin and tiny that I had to squint to see it.

"Yeah," I said sarcastically. "Sounds terrible."

"Anyhow," Ferkle went on, "I found the designer and forced him to tell me the secret to getting in and out of the labyrinth. That wasn't so hard; he was a big weenie. All I had to do was threaten to punch him in the nose, and he started blabbing. It turns out, there's a secret back entrance to get in here. Because the designer didn't want to have to go all the way through the labyrinth and then back out again every time he put a victim in the center. I can show you the way out right now. Ready to go?"

"Yes!" Princess Grace, Belinda, and I yelled all at once.

"Can I come too?" Chad asked.

"I suppose," Ferkle said. "But . . . don't you live here? You're a minotaur, after all."

"Minotaurs don't live in labyrinths!" Chad exclaimed. "They're not our natural habitat! We're half-bull and half-human! We live half the time in homes and half the time in fields! It wasn't even my decision to come in here! That awful king of Extravagancia captured me and stuck me here!"

"Oh," Ferkle said. "Well, then, you should absolutely feel free to come with us." He led the way back through the secret door, taking care to lock it tightly behind him so that none of the bloodthirsty creatures could escape after us.

We now found ourselves in a very different tunnel from the ones that we had been in before. This one was well lit with torches and didn't have any frightening beasts in it. It was also much straighter and more direct than the twisty, confusing tunnels of the labyrinth. And so it wasn't that long a walk at all until we could see daylight ahead.

"Gosh," Belinda said to Princess Grace, sounding kind of depressed. "I guess we didn't have to go through that whole ordeal in the labyrinth after all. We could have just stayed with Ferkle and rescued you the easy way."

"Nonsense," Princess Grace replied. "Because you came the hard way, you arrived just in time to rescue me from those venomous cave snakes. If you'd come the other way, you would have been too late."

"Plus," Chad said, "if you'd come in the easy way, you would have never found me, and I'd still be stuck in the labyrinth. So now I owe you one."

"I guess you're both right," Belinda said. "Whew. I'm glad we didn't have to go through all of that for nothing."

We emerged from the secret tunnel. The exit was hidden behind some bushes surprisingly close to the main entrance of the labyrinth. Three men were gathered there: Prince Ruprecht, Nerlim, and an older man with fine robes and a golden crown.

"That's the king of Extravagancia!" Chad hissed angrily. "The one who put me in the labyrinth!"

We all stayed behind the bushes so they wouldn't notice us. We were close enough to easily overhear them.

"You're sure they won't ever be able to get out of here?" Prince Ruprecht asked the king. "Because even though those knights are young, they are very smart and crafty."

"I promise you they can't escape," the king assured him. "This is the finest labyrinth in the world, and I have filled it with all sorts of bloodthirsty beasts and deadly obstacles. It is exceptionally dastardly and cruel. Especially the chrubble. Ooh! And the cave sharks are also a nice touch."

"Excellent," Nerlim said. "We obviously came to the right place to get rid of those thorns in our sides once and for all." He took a sack out of his pocket. From the jingling noise it made, it sounded as though it was full of golden coins. "Thanks for letting us use it."

"Of course!" the king said, taking the money. "That's what it's here for!"

Overhearing all this made me very angry. I wanted to leap out from my hiding place and punch all three of them in the face. I could tell that Belinda was thinking the same thing. Her fists were clenched, and she was steaming mad.

In fact, she was ready to attack. But I put a hand on her shoulder, stopping her, then whispered, "Don't start any trouble."

"But they deserve trouble!" she whispered back.

"I know," I said. "And they'll get plenty of it. I have a plan." Then I told everyone what it was.

Meanwhile, Prince Ruprecht, Nerlim, and the king of Extravagancia were having a very good time, imagining how miserable the rest of us were.

"This is an ingeniously horrible place," Prince Ruprecht said. "I think I'll use it to get rid of all of my enemies from now on."

"Yes," Nerlim agreed. "It's really quite . . . a-maze-ing."

Even though this was an extremely corny and not very original joke, they all laughed hysterically at it.

"Ho-ho-ho!" Prince Ruprecht chortled.

"Hee-hee-hee!" Nerlim guffawed.

"Har-har-har-har-har . . . AAAAAAAAAAAGGG-GGGGHHHHHHHHH!" the king screamed in terror.

Prince Ruprecht and Nerlim screamed too. Because a terrifying beast was bearing down on them:

I had seated Rover on Chad's head, and now the two of them together looked like a horrible frog-bull combo with a dash of human thrown in. Also, Chad was yelling at the top of his lungs in as scary a voice as he could.

"It's a minotoad!" Prince Ruprecht screamed.

"It's a bullfrog!" Nerlim yelped.

"I don't care what it is!" the king shrieked. "It's coming right for us! Run!"

The three of them fled from Chad and Rover as fast as they could—but the only place they could escape to at the moment was the labyrinth itself. They dashed through the entrance. The portcullis clanged down behind them, locking them inside—although they didn't even notice. They were so scared of Chad and Rover, they just kept on running.

I heard their footsteps echoing for quite some time before they stopped. After that I heard very distant, very frightened voices.

"Do you think we got away from that horrible creature?" Prince Ruprecht asked.

"Yes," Nerlim said. "Although I wasn't paying any attention to where we were going. Does anyone know which way the entrance is?"

"I can't tell," the king said, sounding scared. "It's so dark in here."

"Wait," Ruprecht said, sounding scared as well. "You don't know how to get out of here?"

"It's the finest labyrinth in the world!" the king exclaimed. "No one knows how to get out of it!"

"Oh no!" Nerlim exclaimed. "We're trapped!"

And then the three of them started crying.

I almost felt bad for them.

But not quite.

Mostly, I felt like it was time to go home.

Although there was one *really* scary thing that I still had to do.

CHAPTER FIFTEEN

How I Faced My Greatest Fear

The really scary thing I had to do was *not* to face another bloodthirsty monster.

Or confront another deadly obstacle.

(Thankfully, Ferkle knew a way back to our kingdom that was extremely safe.)

In some ways, what I had to do was even scarier than either of those things.

I had to admit the truth.

I decided that I needed to do it before we got back to Merryland and Princess Grace tried to punish Sir Cumference for something that I had actually done. I waited until after we had dropped Chad off with his relatives, who lived along the way home. (I felt like it would be easier to admit the truth without a minotaur around.)

It turned out he had several other adopted cousins who were half-human and half–other things. They were all very unique but very happy to have their family reunited.

Then, once we had gone a little bit farther, I screwed up my nerve and said, "Bull and Princess Grace. I have something to tell you. Sir Cumference isn't the one who fell asleep at the gates of the castle. It was me."

Then I cringed, waiting for both of them to chew me out.

But they didn't.

"Oh," Belinda said. "Okay."

"You're not angry?" I asked.

"Well, I'm not pleased that you lied and said it was actually Sir Cumference. . . ."

"I only did that because I *thought* you'd be angry," I explained. "Back at the Chasm of the Cave Sharks, you said that *I* should be angry at whoever had fallen asleep at the gates. . . ."

"Really?" Belinda asked. "Well, I was under a lot of stress at the time. Sorry about that."

"No!" I exclaimed. "Stop apologizing to me! *I'm* the one who made the mistake! If I hadn't fallen asleep, Princess Grace would never have ended up with the apples, and then we wouldn't have been in this mess!"

"Actually . . . ," Grace said, looking ashamed, "all this is really *my* fault. *I'm* the one who accepted the bad apples from a suspicious merchant. I know you keep trying to take the blame for me, Tim, but honestly, it was *my* mistake that got us into this mess. Not yours."

"We've *all* made mistakes," Belinda said. "I might have . . . er . . . possibly been the . . . ah . . . one who dropped the twine."[3]

"Oh," I said. It seemed that I should be angry at her for doing this and then lying about it, but I wasn't. Instead, I was pleased she had admitted the truth. So I said, "That's okay. I'm sorry I got angry at you back in the labyrinth."

"And I'm sorry I got angry at *you* for something that was my fault."

Before I knew it, instead of arguing, we were all apologizing to one another and then laughing about the fact that we were being ridiculously apologetic. And then we ended up laughing because Ferkle had put a badger on his head instead of his hat. (He might have been an intelligent

---

3. I knew it!!!!!

village idiot, but doing idiotic things was still part of his job description.)

After that, despite everything that had happened that day, I felt surprisingly good. It was a huge relief to have told the truth—and of course I was pleased to have survived the labyrinth. I was also pleased to be with my good friends. And I had learned a valuable lesson about honesty. (Basically, things will always be better if you tell the truth.)

It wasn't like *all* my problems were taken care of. Sir Vyval and the other knights were still going to be tough on me. And there was always a chance that Prince Ruprecht and Nerlim would escape the labyrinth and be even angrier and more determined to seek revenge on us. And it was olden times, so you never knew when the next plague of dragons was going to crop up.

But for the moment, I was with my friends, and I was happy, so it seems like this is a decent place to say . . .

THE END

Acknowledgments

I am extremely grateful to many, many people for their help with this book.

("Grateful" means really, really, really thankful. Without the help of the people I'm going to list below, this book wouldn't exist. Instead, it would be a whole bunch of weird jokes that I'd be annoying my friends with.)

For starters, I'm grateful to my wonderful illustrator, Stacy Curtis, for bringing my characters and this world to life.

And I'm also grateful to my incredible team at Simon & Schuster: Krista Vitola, Justin Chanda, Lucy Ruth Cummins, Kendra Levin, Catherine Laudone, Anne Zafian, Beth Parker, Lisa Moraleda, Jenica Nasworthy, Tom Daly, Chava Wolin, Chrissy Noh, Devin MacDonald, Brian Murray, Christina Pecorale, Victor Iannone, Emily Hutton, Emily Ritter, Michelle Leo, and Theresa Pang.

Additional gratefulness goes to my amazing fellow

writers (and support group): Sarah Mlynowski, James Ponti, Rose Brock, Julie Buxbaum, Christina Soontornvat, Karina Yan Glaser, Max Brallier, and Gordon Korman.

Even more gratefulness goes to my interns, Emma Chanen, Caroline Curran, and Paola Camacho, as well as Barry and Carole Patmore; Suz, Darragh, and Ciara Howard; and Ronald and Jane Gibbs.

And finally, I could not be more grateful for my amazing children, Dashiell and Violet, who make me laugh and smile and burst with happiness every day. I love you both more than words can say.

About the Author and Illustrator

Stuart Gibbs is the *New York Times* bestselling author of the Charlie Thorne, FunJungle, Moon Base Alpha, Spy School, and Once Upon a Tim series. He has written screenplays, worked on a whole bunch of animated films, developed TV shows, been a newspaper columnist, and researched capybaras (the world's largest rodents). Stuart lives with his family in Los Angeles. You can learn more about what he's up to at stuartgibbs.com.

Stacy Curtis is a *New York Times* bestselling and award-winning illustrator, cartoonist, and printmaker. He has illustrated more than thirty-five children's books, including *Karate Kakapo*, which won the National Cartoonists Society's Book Illustration award. Stacy lives in the Chicago area with his wife, daughter, and two dogs.

About the Author and Illustrator

Stuart Gibbs is the *New York Times* bestselling author of the Charlie Thorne, FunJungle, Moon Base Alpha, Spy School, and Once Upon a Tim series. He has written screenplays, worked on a whole bunch of animated films, developed TV shows, been a newspaper columnist, and researched capybaras (the world's largest rodents). Stuart lives with his family in Los Angeles. You can learn more about what he's up to at stuartgibbs.com.

Stacy Curtis is a *New York Times* bestselling and award-winning illustrator, cartoonist, and printmaker. He has illustrated more than thirty-five children's books, including *Karate Kakapo*, which won the National Cartoonists Society's Book Illustration award. Stacy lives in the Chicago area with his wife, daughter, and two dogs.